Cheese. He's the one with the famous bottom.

His bottom is so famous that we all went on a nationwide tour in this amazing tour bus.

THE FANTASTIC DUMPER ROADSHOW!

AS SEEN ON TV – THE MOST FAMOUS
BOTTOM IN THE WORLD

TRY OUT THE NEW BUMPER DUMPER
DISPOSABLE NAPPY!

And that's when all the trouble started . . .

Jeremy Strong once worked in a bakery, putting the jam into three thousand doughnuts every night. Now he puts the jam in stories instead, which he finds much more exciting. At the age of three, he fell out of a first-floor bedroom window and landed on his head. His mother says that this damaged him for the rest of his life and refuses to take any responsibility. He loves writing stories because he says it is 'the only time you alone have complete control and can make anything happen'. His ambition is to make you laugh (or at least snuffle). Jeremy Strong lives in Somerset with a flying cow and a cat.

Read more about Nicholas's daft family

MY DAD'S GOT AN ALLIGATOR!
MY GRANNY'S GREAT ESCAPE
MY MUM'S GOING TO EXPLODE!
MY BROTHER'S FAMOUS BOTTOM

Are you feeling silly enough to read more?

THE HUNDRED-MILE-AN-HOUR DOG
RETURN OF THE HUNDRED-MILE-AN-HOUR DOG
WANTED! THE HUNDRED-MILE-AN-HOUR DOG

BEWARE! KILLER TOMATOES
CHICKEN SCHOOL
KRAZY KOW SAVES THE WORLD – WELL ALMOST

LAUGH YOUR SOCKS OFF WITH Jeremy STRONG

My Brother's Famous Bottom Gets Pinched!

Illustrated by

Rowan Clifford

PUFFIN

This is especially for Lily

PUFFIN BOOKS

Published by the Penguin Group
Penguin Books Ltd, 80 Strand, London WC2R 0RL, England
Penguin Group (USA) Inc., 375 Hudson Street, New York, New York 10014, USA
Penguin Group (Canada), 90 Eglinton Avenue East, Suite 700, Toronto, Ontario, Canada M4P 2Y3
(a division of Pearson Penguin Canada Inc.)
Penguin Ireland, 25 St Stephen's Green, Dublin 2, Ireland (a division of Penguin Books Ltd)
Penguin Group (Australia), 250 Camberwell Road, Camberwell, Victoria 3124, Australia
(a division of Pearson Australia Group Pty Ltd)
Penguin Books India Pvt Ltd, 11 Community Centre, Panchsheel Park, New Delhi – 110 017, India
Penguin Group (NZ), 67 Apollo Drive, Rosedale, North Shore 0632, New Zealand
(a division of Pearson New Zealand Ltd)
Penguin Books (South Africa) (Pty) Ltd, 24 Sturdee Avenue, Rosebank, Johannesburg 2196, South Africa

Penguin Books Ltd, Registered Offices: 80 Strand, London WC2R 0RL, England

puffinbooks.com

First published 2007
This edition produced for The Book People Ltd,
Hall Wood Avenue, Haydock, St Helens. WA11 9UL
001

Text copyright © Jeremy Strong, 2007
Illustrations copyright © Rowan Clifford, 2007
All rights reserved

The moral right of the author and illustrator has been asserted

Set in 14/23pt MT Baskerville
Made and printed in England by Clays Ltd, St Ives plc

British Library Cataloguing in Publication Data
A CIP catalogue record for this book is available from the British Library

ISBN: 978-0-141-34934-3

www.greenpenguin.co.uk

Penguin Books is committed to a sustainable
future for our business, our readers and our planet.
This book is made from Forest Stewardship
Council™ certified paper.

ALWAYS LEARNING   **PEARSON**

Contents

1 The Dump Truck

We were having breakfast when an explosion of
noise from outside almost blew us off our seats.

PHARRRRPPPP!

It was a gigantic hooter. Mum jumped out of her skin. Dad yelled 'Alien attack!' and vanished beneath the table. The windows almost fell out of their frames and the twins, Cheese and Tomato, burst into tears. Those aren't their real names, of course. They're actually called James and Rebecca but Dad nicknamed them Cheese and Tomato because they were born in the back of a pizza delivery van.

'What on earth is it?' asked Mum, her eyes on stalks. I dashed to the window and there it was – an alien space cruiser.

Of course it wasn't, but it did look like one. It was the shiniest, newest, biggest and most splendid tour bus ever. Giant sparkly letters right along the side said:

THE FANTASTIC DUMPER ROADSHOW!

And under that in smaller sparkly letters it said:

AS SEEN ON TV – THE MOST FAMOUS BOTTOM IN THE WORLD

And under that in still smaller writing, but still just as sparkly, it said:

TRY OUT THE NEW BUMPER DUMPER DISPOSABLE NAPPY!

THE FANTASTIC DUMPER ROADSHOW!
AS SEEN ON TV – THE MOST FAMOUS
BOTTOM IN THE WORLD
TRY OUT THE NEW BUMPER DUMPER
DISPOSABLE NAPPY!

My jaw almost fell off my face, trying to take it all in. Dad and I watched in stunned silence as double doors on the side of the bus slid back with a loud hiss. Mechanical steps automatically unfolded. A trumpet fanfare blasted the air.

PAH! PA-PA-RA-PAH, PA-RAH!!

A big, jolly man stepped down from the bus.
It was Mr Dumper, the King of Throwaway
Nappies.

'I said it was an alien attack,' Dad muttered.

'He's not an alien.'

'If that isn't an alien then my name's not Peter
Pinkle Plumpot.'

'Dad, your name isn't Peter Pinkle Plumpot,' I
told him. 'It's Ron.'

'Oh no,' cried Dad. 'You've discovered my
secret! That must mean I'm your true father! And
what do you know, I think that's David Dumper,
disguised as a creature from outer space.' He
waggled his eyebrows at me. My Dad's as daft as a
dog with two tails. He's great!

'I wonder what he wants?' mused Dad, as Mr
Dumper hammered on our front door.

'He wants to come in,' Mum pointed out. 'Are
you two going to play Dick and Dom with each

other all morning or will you open the door for him?'

'You go, Dick,' said Dad.

'How did I know you'd say that?' I sighed and went to the front door.

David Dumper stood on the doorstep grinning from ear to ear. He threw his arms wide. 'Ah! My favourite family. Now then, where's my fabulous bottom?'

'It's behind you,' said Dad. 'Where else could it be? On your head?'

Mr Dumper burst out laughing and his shoulders heaved like crazy. 'Always playing the clown, eh, Ron?'

Mum gave a little sigh. 'It's not playing, David – Ron *is* a clown,' and Mr Dumper's shoulders heaved with laughter again.

'You know I mean little Cheese. Where is he? Ah, there you are, and Tomato too.' Mr Dumper lifted them up, one on each arm. 'Come on then,

come and see the amazing Bumper Dumper tour
bus. Now then, what do you think?'

'Big,' said Dad.

'Shiny,' I added.

'Noisy,' Mum finished off. 'Your horn almost
broke our windows.'

'I know! Isn't it brilliant?' shouted Mr Dumper.

'I took delivery today and I just had to come round and show you. It's for a new advertising campaign.'

We wandered round the tour bus, while Mr Dumper pointed out all the special lettering, how big the wheels were and all the different gizmos the bus had. There was satellite TV, pull-out beds, an on-board fridge full of drinks and there was even a chocolate fountain! By this time we had been joined by a crowd of onlookers. One of them was making a great deal of noise and seemed to be doing an excellent impression of a human earthquake. It was Mr Tugg, our next-door neighbour.

'You're parked across my driveway!' he shouted through gritted teeth.

'Keep your hair on, old man,' said Dad. 'Oh, you haven't got any. Never mind.'

'You're parked across my driveway!' repeated Mr Tugg, his face turning purple.

Dad beamed at him and clicked his fingers.

'You've said that twice. Is it the chorus of a song? How does the rest of it go? Oh, I know – *the wheels on the bus go round and* – no, I can tell by the look on your face it's not that one.'

'You're parked across my driveway!' screamed Mr Tugg for the third time, hopping about like a frog in a frying pan.

'Did you want to go somewhere in your car?' asked Mr Dumper politely.

'Not at the moment but, but, but – you're parked across –'

'– the driveway,' Mr Dumper finished. 'Listen, I shall be gone very shortly. I just need to talk to your lovely neighbours for five minutes.'

'Lovely neighbours?' choked Mr Tugg, staring at my dad with horror. 'They're not lovely. They're a nightmare. Do you know what they've got in their back garden? A goat! And cabbages, and a tortoise called Schwarzenegger.'

'Schumacher,' Mum corrected quietly. She put

an arm round Mr Tugg's shoulder and gently helped him towards his own house. 'The tour bus will be gone soon, I promise. Why don't you ask Mrs Tugg to make you a nice cup of tea?'

Mr Dumper watched as Mr Tugg disappeared back into his house. 'Is he always like that?' he asked and we nodded glumly. Mr Dumper seemed puzzled. 'Do you really have a goat and a tortoise?'

Mum explained that we grew most of our own food at the back of the house. 'The goat gives us milk, which we turn into yoghurt and cheese.'

'And the tortoise? What does that do?' asked Mr Dumper.

'Security,' said Dad. 'He's our security officer. Top man, too – we haven't had a single cabbage stolen since he's been on patrol. Now, what's this tour bus in aid of? Why have you brought it round here to show us?'

'And why does it say: AS SEEN ON TV – THE MOST FAMOUS BOTTOM IN THE WORLD on it?' added Mum.

'Ah, glad you asked. I have a terrific plan. Ever since your baby Cheese appeared on telly to advertise my nappies he's become a star. My idea is that we take Cheese round the whole country, appearing in different towns and showing off my new Bumper Dumper range of disposable nappies. It will be like what he did in the TV advert, only more personal. People will flock to see the real Cheese.'

'Like a model?' I suggested. That really impressed Dad.

'You're right, Nick. Fancy that, my son, a model. Presumably that makes me a model father.'

'More like a model idiot,' Mum corrected. A frown passed across her face. 'The thing is, Mr Dumper, you can't just drag Cheese round the country. What about the rest of the family? One of us will have to go with him.'

Mr Dumper smiled. 'Cheese won't be on his own. The tour is for all of us.'

'All of us?' repeated Mum.

'Even me?' I asked, and Mr Dumper nodded. 'Cool! Can we? Can we really go? Will we be staying in hotels and everything?' My head was bursting with excitement.

David Dumper nodded and stood there watching our faces. Dad looked at Mum. Mum looked at Dad. I looked at them. They looked at me.

'I don't see why not,' said Mum. 'It's the school holidays.'

'I don't go to school,' Dad pointed out.

'Don't be ridiculous, Ron. I mean Nicholas.'

'Oh,' coughed Dad, and he tried to look serious. 'Yes, of course. Nicholas.'

This was the most brilliant thing ever. A roadshow, starring the whole family! And then my heart went dead. What about our goat, Rubbish? I'm the only one who can milk her, apart from Granny's husband, Lancelot, who doesn't live with us, so he can't do it. And if she didn't get milked she'd, well, I suppose she'd probably explode eventually, like a four-legged milk-bomb. I sank into gloom. Along comes this amazing chance to stay in hotels and whizz about the country in a flashy tour bus like a superstar, and now I shall have to stay at home to look after a stinky goat.

2 Granny's Magic

It's quite calming, milking a goat. It gives you time
to think. Your brain goes kind of dreamy and all
sorts of ideas pop into your head, at least they do
into mine, and I got three ideas for sorting out
Rubbish almost immediately.

1. A milking machine.
2. A robot.
3. A babysitter.

I soon realized that Plan 1 wouldn't work.
Any kind of milking machine would have to
be connected to Rubbish all the time because
there'd be nobody there to fix it on or take it off
her. Rubbish wanders about a lot and she also
has a habit of trying to eat anything that comes

anywhere near her, so I don't think an automatic machine would last long.

Plan 2 was to build a robot, but how would a robot know where to find the goat? (Note Plan 1 and the wandering.) Sometimes Rubbish was in the back garden. Sometimes she came in the house, and sometimes

she tried to annoy Mr Tugg as much as possible by creeping into his garden and eating his top notch, grade one, velvety green lawn.

'It doesn't have a single weed in it,' he told my dad, very proudly, the other week.

'But, Mr Tugg,' my dad answered, 'grass *is* a weed. Every single blade of your lawn is a bit of weed. Your lawn is nothing but weed.'

'You won't make me get cross,' Mr Tugg said, gritting his teeth yet again. 'I know you're trying to wind me up, but it won't happen.'

'Weed World,' murmured Dad, as if he was talking to himself.

'La la la,' sang Mr Tugg. 'Can't hear you! Tra la la . . .'

'Planet Weed.'

'IT'S NOT WEED
– IT'S LAWN!' Mr Tugg
suddenly roared.

LA LA LA

'LAWN spelt W-E-E-D.'

I think that Mr Tugg
should be connected to
the local power station.
He produces enough steam from his ears to make
his own electricity.

Then there was Plan 3: get a babysitter – well,
not exactly a babysitter, more of a goat sitter.
Guess what? There's no such thing. I searched in
Yellow Pages, which gives you phone numbers for
just about everything. I looked up GOAT and
the closest thing was GO-KARTS, which was no
use at all. My heart sank into even deeper gloom.
Mum tried to reassure me.

'We'll think of something.'

'I've tried asking Dad already,' I moaned and
Mum rolled her eyes.

'It's no good asking him. You know perfectly well that your dad can't do Sensible. He can only do Daft.'

At that point there was a rumbling roar from outside the house, which was a sure sign that Granny and Lancelot had arrived on one of their motorbikes. They've got three altogether. There are HIS and HERS bikes for when they ride solo, while number three bike has a sidecar attached so they can take extras like me for a spin. They can even fit the sidecar with a double baby seat and they take Cheese and Tomato out sometimes. You should see the twins with their tiny goggles! They look like frogs.

As soon as Granny came in she could see something was wrong. 'Oh, Nicholas, you do look down in the dumps.'

'He's worried about the goat,' Mum told her.

'Your coat? You haven't left it at school again, have you?'

In case you hadn't guessed, Granny is a bit
deaf, but not all the time. It seems to come and
go. It usually comes when someone tries to tell her
something she doesn't want to know. However,
she can hear perfectly well if you mention
chocolate, or a cup of tea, or snooker – which are
three of her favourite things.

'It's Rubbish,' I told her and explained
everything.

Granny didn't seem to think there was any
problem at all. 'All we need is a wooden spoon,'
she said.

'Really?'

'Yes. Ah, there's one in this drawer. Nicholas, you stand there and keep still while I do something special with this spoon.' Mum and I looked at Granny with bewilderment. 'Go on,' said Granny sharply. 'Stand over there.'

Granny took the spoon and waved it round her head several times. 'Nicholas, Nicholas,' she cried, 'you SHALL go to the ball!' She put the spoon back in the kitchen drawer and smiled. 'There,' she said. 'All done.'

I looked at Mum, just in case she knew what was going on, because I certainly didn't. What ball? I didn't want to go to any ball – that would mean dancing. Urgh! Mum made faces at me as if to suggest that Granny was going a wee bit mad. As for Granny herself, she just sighed.

'Isn't it obvious? That was my Fairy Grandmother's magic wand I was waving. Rubbish can come and stay with Lancelot and me. Lance is the only other person who can milk her. It'll only be for a week, won't it?'

I hurtled across to Granny and threw my arms round her. 'Granny, that is definitely magic. You are the bee's knees!'

There was a loud protest from behind. 'Hey there, young man, that's my babe you're hugging. Put her down at once. How dare you!'

It was Lancelot, of course, grinning from ear

to ear, and I had to hug him too. He's really nice.
You'd never think he is actually Mr Tugg's dad.
He is! Just look at the pair of them! There's Mr
Tugg, who's forty and practically bald and about
as friendly as a cactus with bad breath, and then
there's Lancelot, who is sixty-five, wears a leather
jacket with fringes and
has so much hair he ties
it in a ponytail.

'Rubbish will have
a top time with us,'
Lancelot said. 'You
won't need to worry
about a thing. Anyway,
what's going on? Where are you lot off to?' We
had to run through the whole business about the
roadshow.

You see, my baby brother Cheese has got the
most famous bottom in the country. At least
that's what my dad says. You know that advert on

television for Dumpers disposable nappies? And you know that little baby you see crawling across the floor in the advert, wiggling his bare bum? That's Cheese – my little brother! He even got on the TV news once. Millions of viewers saw him.

Dad watched proudly as Cheese wriggled across the floor. 'That's my boy! What a bottom! Of course, he gets his good looks from his father.'

'Ron, all you can see is his bottom,' Mum answered, slapping a clean nappy on Cheese's rear end and letting him wander off again.

'That's what I mean,' Dad nodded. 'I have a lovely bottom too.'

'I can't believe we're having this conversation,' sighed Mum. 'Can we talk about something else,

POO!

please?'

'Poo!' shouted Tomato, because it's about the only word she knows.

'No,' said Mum. 'Not poo. I've told you before, Tomato. It's not polite. Goodness gracious, all we ever seem to talk about in this house nowadays is poo and bottoms. I'm fed up with it all.'

'Bottoms are very important,' announced Dad

seriously.

'No they're not.'

'Oh yes. If you didn't have a bottom your legs would have nothing to join on to. So, no bottom means no legs either. Where would you be then? You wouldn't be able to walk. You'd have to get round some other way. I've got it! If you ate enough beans you could produce enough downward air thrust to turn yourself into a hovercraft. It might be a bit whiffy, that's all.'

'I'm not listening to any more of your revolting conversation, Ron. Do talk about something normal just for once, please – and Nicholas, Cheese is trying to escape upstairs again. Go and get him before he falls.'

I launched yet another Search and Rescue Operation on Cheese. He's always vanishing off somewhere, especially now that he's toddling. Tomato is too, but Cheese is the quickest. He can do nought-to-waddle-speed in two seconds flat.

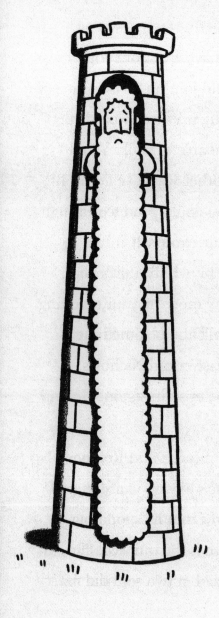

Lancelot wanted to know if Cheese would have to sign autographs. Mum laughed.

'Don't be silly, Lance, he's one and a half. He's nowhere near writing yet.'

Dad beamed. 'There's more than one way to leave an autograph. He could leave his mark some other way.'

Mum eyed Dad warily. 'I know I shall be very sorry I asked this, but just what did you have in mind?'

'He could do a wee on a nappy, or a –'

'NO, RON! NO WAY! I knew you'd come up with something foul. You are a revolting, disgusting man who should be shut away in a very tall tower for umpteen years and only fed with raw potatoes and rice pudding.'

'I don't like rice pudding,' said Dad.

'You're not supposed to like it. That's your punishment for being so disgusting.'

'Huh! Well, I think rice pudding is a lot more disgusting than Cheese's –'

'RON!' bellowed Mum. Dad looked at me and winked. I couldn't help smiling back at him.

'And you're just as bad, Nicholas. Don't encourage your father.' Mum turned on Granny. 'It's your fault. He's your son. It was the way you brought him up.'

'Oh no, dear,' protested Granny. 'Don't blame me. He fell on his head when he was two. He's never been the same since. Besides, you did marry him. You didn't have to.'

'I didn't realize what a weird family he came from,' Mum said darkly. Dad went across to her and draped one arm round her shoulders.

'You should be proud. We all should. We have produced a superstar son, or at least a super-bottom, and I think that's wonderful, don't you?'

Mum softened. She smiled. 'Of course I do,

you daft doughnut.' She leaned closer, puckered her lips and planted a noisy kiss on his mouth.

I pulled a face. 'Mum? Dad? Do you have to? I'm only eleven. You shouldn't do that until after nine o'clock at night.'

Everyone stopped and looked at me, even Cheese and Tomato. Mum and Dad chorused, 'Ooooooh!'

'Poo!' went Tomato, and I nodded.

'Exactly. That's just what I think too.'

3 A Life of Luxury

We're on the road! It's brilliant, apart from Dad's
endless singing. I've lost count of the times he's
been through 'The Wheels on the Bus'. Then
he started on 'Ten Green Bottles' which he soon
turned into 'Ten Dirty Nappies'.

The tour bus is fantastic. It's got a big television
and also DVD players built into the backs of
seats. There's even a shower and toilet, and a
mini-kitchen. You could live on board if you
wanted to. Just think, you could go anywhere in
the world and you'd have your house with you.
And I haven't even told you the most astonishing
thing about it. There's a secret room! You press
a button and a big section slides out from one
side of the tour bus and creates an extra room.
Amazing! And then you press another button and

the outer wall rolls up into the roof, so the room turns into a kind of stage.

'That's where we do the roadshow from,' Mr Dumper explained.

'Cool!'

Dad agreed. 'Yeah, cool, man,' he said, holding out his hand to me. 'Give me six!'

'Um, it's five,' I muttered.

'I know,' he blustered. 'But this tour bus is cooler than cool, so it's gone up to six. OK?'

We were on the tour bus for hours and I was just beginning to get bored when we arrived at our first hotel. I've never been in a hotel before. I thought we'd be in bedrooms next to each other, but Mr Dumper had booked a suite for us, which is like having your own miniature house. It's got three bedrooms, a bathroom and a living room. There's a fridge full of chocolate and drinks and stuff. When we first walked in there was a bottle of champagne sticking out of an ice bucket.

'Ooh la la!' cried Dad, pulling it from the bucket.

'Poo la la!' copied Tomato.

Ooh la la

Poo la la

CHA

'Hmmm. I'm not sure *Poo la la* has quite the same ring to it,' muttered Mum.

I don't think Dad has opened many champagne bottles. He struggled furiously, gripping it between

his thighs, twisting and yanking and grunting
away like a gorilla with bellyache.

'Try undoing
the wire round it,'
suggested Mum.

'Oh. Yes. Good
idea.'

He got the
wire off and then
began twisting and
yanking all over
again. 'It's no good.
It's not going to –'

BANG!

The cork exploded out of the bottle, hit the
ceiling, ricocheted off, hit the opposite wall, went
whizzing off and hit a big display of flowers on
the table. They crashed over and water flooded
the floor. While we all stood and stared at that the
champagne foamed out of the bottle and started a

bubble flood of its own.

'What?' said Dad, looking at Mum, who was giving him one of her '*Why did I ever marry you?*' looks.

'I didn't say a word,' murmured Mum.

We all had a glass of champagne, apart from Cheese and Tomato, of course, who are too young. Mind you, it didn't stop Cheese from toddling over to the mini champagne flood. He paddled in it a bit, then sat down, dabbed his fingers in and sucked them. Yuk!

I only had half a glass but it was great. The bubbles go right up your nose – at least mine did and I spluttered them back into the glass.

'You're not supposed to sniff it,' Mum laughed.

'Couldn't help it.'

'Hey, come in here!' called Dad from the

bathroom and we went in to see what he was up to. You should see our bathroom – it's gigantic. It's about three times as big as our front room at home. The bath is right in the middle, just standing there on four fat metal lion's feet. There's a giant silver shower head hanging above it. Dad was already trying out the tub, lying back in it with all his clothes on.

Mum looked around and fingered the thick white towels. 'It's no wonder some rich people spend their lives living in hotels. If I were rich enough, I think I might. This is complete luxury.'

Dad clicked his fingers at her. 'Slave – scrub my back,' he ordered. Mum looked down at him and her eyes glinted.

'I wonder what this tap does?' she hinted.

'No, you wouldn't, don't you dare, if you turn that tap on I'll – aaaaargh!'

It was the shower, and the water was cold. Mum smiled sweetly at him. 'Oh, so that's what that tap does. It makes you jump. And very wet.'

Dad stood up, dripping with water. 'I shall get you for this,' he said, stepping out of the bath and moving towards her.

'Ron, no, keep away, don't you dare touch me – you're soaking. Ron, don't come any closer or I'll scream. Eeeeeeee!'

Dad grabbed Mum round the waist and gave

her the biggest hug he could, while she struggled and squirmed.

'Urrgh, you're all wet!' she complained. I thought it was hilarious until I realized that they'd stopped fighting each other and were looking at me.

'He's laughing at us,' said Mum.

'And he's dry,' added Dad. 'Come on!'

And the next thing I knew I was being hugged between them, so I got wet too. Then David Dumper came in to see us.

'You know, usually, people get undressed before they have a shower,' he said, eyeing our wet clothes.

'Ah, so that's what

we did wrong,' Dad answered.

'I came in to remind you it's the first show tomorrow, so I'll see you at breakfast, eight o'clock sharp.'

I was quite glad to get to bed in the end. It had been a long day, and quite an exciting one. I wish you could have seen my bed. It was almost as big as the whole of my bedroom at home. There was

 a chocolate on my pillow too, a really nice one. I asked Mum and Dad if they'd put it there, but no, it was something the hotel did to welcome their guests. I could really get used to this life of luxury!

4 The Big Babies

What a day! It's been really weird. We got
invaded by giant babies. We did! There were
three of them, two men and a woman. They
were wearing giant throwaway nappies and had
dummies stuck in their mouths. They made such
a fuss it was a bit scary actually. Everyone was

shouting and rushing about. Cheese and Tomato
started crying and the audience began to boo.

We were doing our first show. Mr Dumper
had parked the Flying Dumper in the market
square. There was quite a crowd gathered by the
tour bus, waiting to see what was going on. Mr
Dumper made several announcements over the
loudspeakers.

'See the most famous bottom in the world – on
show in ten minutes' time!'

Another one was: 'Try the new range of
fabulous Dumper disposable nappies – Bumper
Dumpers, for the more active child!'

And after that: 'You've seen him on TV, you've
seen him on the news – now see him for real
– the star of the show – Cheese and his fabulous
bottom – the world's number one bum!'

'That's pushing it a bit, isn't it?' complained
Dad. 'What about my bum? It isn't at all bad, you
know.'

Mum punched him. I don't
mean she knocked him out
– it was a play punch.
'You don't like it when
Cheese gets all the
attention. You want to
be the star, don't you?'

Dad shrugged and
pretended he didn't care.
'I'm just saying that other people have
nice bottoms too. I have always thought yours is
lovely, for example.'

'Flattery will get you everywhere,' blushed
Mum. 'What about poor Tomato? Her bottom
is just as nice as Cheese's but she's never given
a chance. Nicholas, pass me that Bumper
Dumper nappy, will you? I've got to get Cheese
ready for the show.'

'Will we be on stage too?' I asked. I was
beginning to think like Mum and Dad. Cheese

got all the attention. What about the rest of us?
We're a family – there are five of us – seven if
you count Granny and Lancelot. But it's Cheese
this and Cheese that. He even gets fan mail. He's
a year and a half old, and he gets fan mail! This
came the other day.

Finn? That's a boy's
name, isn't it? Anyhow,
Cheese gets loads of
stuff like that. Most are
from kids but he gets

Deer Cheez,
I luv your bttm
plez marry me.
luv and kisses,
Finn

mail from old ladies too. Sometimes they send
photos of themselves. It's a strange world!

The rest of the family get left out. I know it's kind
of David Dumper to take the whole family with him
and pay for everything, but it's only Cheese that
goes on stage, and all he ever does is crawl around a
bit and show his bottom from time to time. How can
you be famous for something like that?

So I was getting a bit fed up and then it was

time for Cheese to strut his stuff and Mr Dumper took him on stage. The crowd screamed and yelled as if Cheese was a pop star. Mr Dumper began to tell the crowd about the new range of nappies and how wonderful they were and that was when we got invaded by the giant babies.

I have no idea where they came from but suddenly they were rushing across the stage, shouting and waving big placards.

'What's going on?' shouted Dad, picking
Cheese up to protect him.

'No idea!' Mr Dumper yelled back, just as the
microphone was yanked from his hand by one of
the giant babies, who now began bellowing at the
crowd.

'Over eight million nappies are thrown away
every day! Each nappy takes five hundred years
to decompose. That's Bad News for Planet
Earth. Use your common sense and put natural

nappies on your baby – nappies that can be
washed and used again. Join the eco-revolution.
Save the world and use natural nappies. We are
the Natural Nappy Freedom Front – double N,
double F!'

'You mean double daft!' yelled the crowd. 'Get
off and go home to your cots, you big babies!'

'Someone call the police. They should be
locked up.'

And then they were gone. They leaped down
from the stage and vanished almost as quickly as
they'd arrived. I caught a glimpse of them a few
seconds later making their
escape, on skateboards.

For a few moments everyone was quiet as they gathered their senses. Then a chant went up. 'We want Cheese! We want more Cheese!'

'And you shall have more Cheese!' roared Mr Dumper triumphantly, as he held my little brother above his head. And you know what? Mr Dumper sold every single one of his new disposable nappies. The Double N Double F had done a fat lot of good. What a trio of twits.

On the way back to the hotel I asked Dad if throwaway nappies really did take five hundred years to decompose.

'No. It's actually five hundred and seven, plus a few days.'

'I'm being serious, Dad.'

'No good asking me then,' he admitted.

I tried Mr Dumper and he shook his head a couple of times. 'I have no idea, Nicholas, but every single one of my new nappies got sold. What a fantastic day!'

I sat back in my seat. What did the giant baby say? Eight million nappies a day taking five hundred years to decompose. Was that really true? It didn't sound particularly fantastic to me.

5 Today Will Be Squidgy

When we got to the hotel there was an argument
taking place at Reception. It was difficult to hear
what was going on because four of the quarrellers
were dogs. It's true – there were four tiny dogs,
and though they were small they made as much
noise as a monkey house. They yapped and
yipped and kept jumping up and down on the
end of their leads as if their legs were mini pogo
sticks. They had
glittery collars
and were busily
leaping over
each other and
tying themselves
up in knots.

'My dogs go

everywhere with me,' the woman shouted. 'They always have a bed to sleep in. I want a room with two beds, one for me and one for my poochy-poos.'

'I'm sorry, madam,' said the receptionist. 'We don't allow dogs on the beds.'

'Are you suggesting my dogs are dirty?' the woman snapped back, and so it went on.

Mum bent down and whispered in my ear. 'I'm sure I know that woman, Nicholas. Isn't she on television?'

I looked harder. Yes, Mum was right, but who

was it? I tried to squeeze the answer out of my brain.

'Are you all right, Nick?' asked Dad. 'Have you got a headache?'

'Dad, I'm thinking.'

'Oh. Is that what thinking looks like?'

'I know who it is! It's Kristal Gaze, the astrologer. You know, Mum – *Star Daze, with Kristal Gaze* – the one where she looks at your star sign and says what's going to happen to you.'

'So it is. Well, I forecast that the poor receptionist is going to have a bad day today. Just listen to that woman – and those dogs.'

They were making an awful fuss. 'I insist my dogs have a bed,' yelled Kristal, leaning right across the counter to snarl at the receptionist. 'I know your type. You're Scorpio, aren't you? Born to cause trouble, that's what. You can't possibly be helpful, can you? All I want is a bed for my dogs. And a ground-floor room with a view of the river.'

The receptionist turned white. 'I'm sorry, madam, but there isn't a river.'

'THEN GET ONE IMMEDIATELY!' roared Kristal.

Dad muttered to us. 'The woman's barking mad.'

'It's the dogs that are barking, Dad.'

'Ha ha. I hope our room isn't anywhere near hers.'

We couldn't tear ourselves away. It was both horrible and fascinating at the same time. Kristal Gaze was doing a very good imitation of Mr Tugg moving towards the earthquake stage.

'Listen to me, you silly girl, my horoscope says I

must sleep near running water. It helps to clean the spirit channels and, good grief, my spirit channels are going to need a sea-going dredger to clean them after this.'

'I'm ever so sorry, madam, but there is no river. You could leave your bath tap running instead.'

Kristal Gaze swung round and gazed in despair at the other people waiting in Reception. 'Run the bath tap? The woman's an idiot.' She turned back to the poor receptionist, who was almost in tears. 'Get me the manager. I insist on speaking to the manager.'

'What a bully,' Mum said flatly.

The manager arrived and the first thing he did was ask Kristal Gaze to step into his office. He was sure the problem could be sorted out. Kristal followed him down the corridor, along with her four dogs, and all five of them were still yapping like crazy.

'Show's over,' Dad muttered. 'I hope the

manager tells Kristal Gaze and her dogs to go jump in the river.'

'Dad, there isn't a river, remember?'

'Then go and get one, immediately,' Dad chuckled.

Mum had gone across to the reception desk. 'Don't pay any attention to that woman,' Mum told the receptionist. 'She's just a bully. Some of these people you see on television think they're so special, but they're no better than the rest of us.'

She reached across the counter and patted the woman's hand. The receptionist nodded and

sniffed. She was too choked to reply. Mum gave
her an encouraging smile and came back to us.
My mum's like that. She's great.

As we headed for our rooms I asked Mum
and Dad if they knew what star signs they were.
Mum said she was Libra, the Scales, and Dad was
Capricorn, the Goat.

'Do you hear that,
Nick?' said Dad. 'The
Goat. My star sign is
Rubbish!'

'It certainly is,' sighed
Mum. 'And you're
Scorpio, Nicholas. That means you are supposed
to be creative and clever and a bit of a slyboots.'

I grinned. That sounded pretty good to me. I
liked the idea of being clever and cunning. 'What
about Cheese and Tomato? What sign are they?'

Dad stopped dead, facing us, his eyes wide. His
voice went all mysterious. 'They were born under

the Sign of Pizza,' he pronounced, very slowly. Mum burst out laughing.

'I'll ask Kristal what the future is for people born under the Sign of Pizza,' she said. 'That should give her something to think about.'

I lifted Tomato on to my shoulders for a ride.

'So what do you think your future is, Tomato?' I asked. She gurgled back at me.

'Poo pants!'

Poo pants!

'Here we go again,' moaned Mum.

'Actually, she is a bit whiffy, Mum. I think she really has got poo pants.'

'I predict her nappy needs changing,' said Dad, waggling one finger. 'The Sign of Pizza says today will be squidgy.'

Mum gathered Tomato into her arms. 'Every day is squidgy when you have small children. Come on, into the bathroom. Let's get them sorted out.'

If you ask me it's pretty easy to predict what babies are going to do. You certainly know when they've done it. Yuk!

6 Pinched!

I had a bad dream last night, which is not
surprising when you think about the day we'd
had. I was being chased by giant babies and
dwarf dogs. The giant babies were hurling
disposable nappies at me. I was running to escape

through a marsh made of baby food. I think it
might have been stewed apples. It was horrible,
gloopy stuff that sucked at my feet and wouldn't
let them go.

The dwarf dogs,
who were also wearing
nappies, seemed able to
bounce across it on their
pogo legs. The giant babies were closing in on
me. They were slurping on fat dummies and as
they got closer the dummies came shooting out of
their mouths at me. There was no escape. I was
going to die, bombed with nappies and riddled
with dummies.

I woke up, sweating all over. For a moment
I wondered where I was. Then I heard loud
yapping from somewhere not far off. It was
Kristal Gaze's pesky dogs, and it was 2.00 a.m.! I
slumped back on to my pillow and tried to sleep
but the dogs went on and on – yap, yap, yap. The

noise disturbed Cheese and he began to whimper quietly. Then Tomato started and soon they were both crying.

I got up, took Cheese from his cot and cuddled him, trying to shush him quiet, but the yapping wouldn't stop. It was the dogs that needed to shut

up. Mum wandered in sleepily, with her hair all over the place. She yawned crossly, picked up

Tomato and now we were both pacing the room, jiggling a baby on one shoulder and trying to get them back to sleep, but they went on crying.

'This is ridiculous,' muttered Mum. 'We should ring the manager and complain about the noise.'

Even as Mum spoke the telephone in our room jangled. Mum looked at it in surprise for a second and then picked it up.

'What!' she shouted down the phone. 'You must be joking! How dare she complain! You tell Kristal Gaze it was her dogs that woke the twins in the first place. They wouldn't be crying if it hadn't been for her stupid, wretched dogs.' Mum slammed the phone back down on the table. Oh well, no prizes for guessing what that was about. It was another ten minutes before the dogs were quiet and the babies stopped crying immediately. They were so tired. We all were – apart from Dad, who just snored through the whole thing.

'You can tell he was born under the sign of the Goat, can't you?' said Mum, as she headed back to bed. I wasn't sure. I've no idea if goats snore or not.

We were still really tired when the alarm went off in the morning but we couldn't hang about because we had to get on the bus and drive for an hour to a different town, although we'd be coming back to the same hotel for another night.

'And if that Kristal Gaze lets her dogs yap tonight I can promise you at least one murder will take place,' hissed Mum. 'And I shall start with the biggest.'

'I never heard anything,' said Dad, wondering what all the fuss was about. 'What?' he asked, noticing the black looks Mum and I were giving him. 'What have I done now?'

'Doesn't matter, Dad. Forget it.'

Mr Dumper came and joined us. He hadn't heard any yapping either and told us he'd slept like a baby.

'I wish our babies had,' Mum shot back at him.

'They're so cute,' smiled Mr Dumper, and he patted Tomato's head. 'And how is Miss Curly-Top this morning?' he asked.

'Poo pants,' spluttered Tomato, spraying out a mouthful of cereal at the same time.

'No, Tomato. You say *I'm very well, thank you for asking.*'

'My fault,' said Mr Dumper. 'Never ask a baby a question when they're busy eating. Now then, are we all ready for the show?'

'Same as yesterday?' asked Dad.

'Exactly, and let's hope we have another Bumper Dumper sale on our hands. I can't tell you how pleased I am with the way things are going.'

I chewed my lip. Every time he mentioned nappies all I could think of was eight million of them being thrown away every day, and that was just in Britain. Imagine what it would be worldwide. Awesome. I was beginning to see a different Mr Dumper, although he looked jolly and happy and he certainly made things fun for us.

Before we met him we were scraping pennies together. That's why we'd started producing our own food in the back garden. But since Mr Dumper had made Cheese into the baby that sold his nappies, things were a lot better. What's more, here he was taking us all on the amazing Dumper Tour AND putting us all up in posh hotels – even if they did have yappy dogs.

But his Dumpers are part of a nappy mountain that will go on growing and will take at least five hundred years before it even starts to decompose. Does Mr Dumper know that? And if he does, is he going to do anything about it?

Big questions, and I'm only eleven, so don't expect me to answer them. All I know is, it worries me, and I think maybe it should be worrying him. But if he stops making Dumpers, then he won't need Cheese, and if he doesn't need Cheese he won't need us and Cheese won't get paid and we'll be back to scraping pennies.

My brain was beginning to get red hot with all that thinking. It was a good thing we had to busy

ourselves packing the bus. It took my mind off the big stuff. It's astonishing how much you have to remember to take with you when you've got a baby – and we've got two.

We ended up parked outside a shiny, new

shopping mall for the second show of the tour. Mr
Dumper and Cheese were planning to do three
short sessions at half-hour intervals.

'I've quadrupled the supply of Dumpers,' he
told us, rubbing his hands together. 'I'm sure
they're going to sell like hot cakes.'

He was right. I guess the crowd just love a
cute little baby and Cheese was being extra cute,
even if he had had a rough night. He giggled
and gurgled and the crowd oohed and aahed.
Meanwhile I kept an eye out for giant babies but
there was nothing odd going on anywhere. The
second show went just as well. Mr Dumper was
shifting loads of nappies.

'Isn't this great!' he beamed.

'Eight million, two hundred and seventeen,' I
murmured back.

'What?'

'Doesn't matter,' I said weakly. I asked Mum
if I could go off and explore for a bit. I'd had

8,000,217

BIG
DUD

enough of nappies for one day.

'Half an hour,' said Mum. 'I want you back here before the last show finishes. Here, take my mobile in case there are any problems.'

I nodded. Typical Mum – she was always worrying that I'd be kidnapped by aliens or something daft. I wandered off into the mall. It was pretty boring, all clothing and fancy electrical stuff I couldn't possibly afford. I think I had about fifty pence in my pocket. I couldn't even find a sweet shop so in the end I shuffled back to the tour bus.

As I came out of the mall I heard a load of yelling and the roar of an engine. People were scattering in all directions. At first I couldn't make out what was going on, and then I saw the tour bus.

HOW!

It was coming straight towards me at high speed. What on earth was happening? I jumped up and down, frantically waving my arms.

'Stop! It's me! Don't go without me!'

The tour bus didn't stop. It carried on hurtling towards me. *PHARRRRPPP!* went the horn. I raced to one side, tripping over my own feet and rolling in the dust. I looked up just in time to see the tour bus whoosh past and a surge of hot air almost blew my T-shirt off.

I'd seen them. I'd seen Mr Dumper and Mum and Tomato at one of the windows. And I'd seen the driver too – a giant baby. My family had just been stolen by the Natural Nappy Freedom Front!

7 What Now?

It wasn't me who'd been kidnapped after all – it was Mum and the rest of the family. I stood there in a daze, watching the tour bus vanish in a cloud of dust. All I could think was – what's happening? Why have the Double N Double F kidnapped my family? No, it couldn't be *kid*-napping. The babies were kids, but Mum and Dad were grown-ups, so I guess they'd just been mum-and-dad-napped.

I tried hard to think sensibly. Better ring the police. I got out the mobile and began dialling. A horrible thought made me stop at once. If the police found me without my parents they'd probably stick me in a Children's Home, or maybe they'd say my parents didn't look after me properly and take me away from them and give me to some other parents THAT I DIDN'T

EVEN KNOW!

I wanted to shout out and tell everyone, but that would cause the same trouble. Some adult would call the police and before I knew it I'd be taken into care. But I had to do something. What?

Of course! I could ring *them*! I dialled Dad's mobile. There was a pause, then a voice said: *'This phone is not switched on. Please leave a message.'*

I switched off. What message could I leave

Dad? 'Guess what? You've been dad-napped!' Even he must know that by now. Who else could I ring? The answer came to me like an elephant falling out of the sky. Granny and Lancelot. They would know what to do. I listened to the ringing

at the other end. Come on, answer, please, please, please answer!

71

'Hello?' It was Granny.

'Granny, everyone's been kidnapped!'

'Is that Nicholas? Every bun is what, dear?'

'Not buns – every*one*. Mum and Dad have been stolen by giant babies and they've taken Cheese and Tomato too, and Mr Dumper. They've been driven away on the tour bus and I'm on my own and I don't know what to do.'

'Why are your parents stealing babies? They've got two of their own already. Isn't that enough?'

'Granny, PLEASE don't be all deaf and muddled now.'

'You sound upset, Nicholas. Is it because of the giant buns? Did the babies eat them?'

'THERE AREN'T ANY BUNS! Granny, go and get Lancelot.'

'I think you'd better speak to Lancelot,' said Granny. I heard her passing the phone across to Lancelot and telling him I was upset as there weren't any buns because some babies had taken

them but she didn't know why I was ringing because there was nothing they could do about it. 'You speak to him,' she finished. 'Tell him he can have some buns when he comes home.'

'Nicholas?' Lancelot's deep voice was so reassuring I almost broke into tears. I spilled the whole story as quickly as I could.

'Are you OK?' he checked.

'I'm not hurt or anything.'

'Good. We'll be with you as fast as we can. Your gran will ring when we get near.'

'Does she have to?' I asked weakly. 'Can't you ring instead?' I didn't think I could go through another conversation with Granny like the last one I'd had. Lancelot chuckled.

'Good lad. Keep your spirits up and don't worry. See you in an hour or so.'

I found a bench and sat down. I felt exhausted and I hadn't really done anything except make a phone call. I gazed around. It seemed so normal it was eerie. The shoppers were back looking in shop windows, pushing prams, eating burgers – all the everyday things you see on every high street in every town. It was almost as if the tour bus had not only vanished from sight, it had vanished from their memories, as if nothing had ever happened at all. I was the only person left on the planet who knew THE TRUTH!

Apart from Mum and Dad, of course. And Cheese and Tomato. And Mr Dumper. And the Natural Nappy Freedom Front. And Granny and

Lancelot. But apart from them, it was just me.

And here's another odd thing. Have you noticed how an hour sometimes feels like an hour, and sometimes it feels like about five minutes, and sometimes it feels like a week? Waiting for Lancelot and Granny felt like a year, but at last I heard the unmistakable roar of their motorbike. I stood on the bench to get a better view and soon saw them moving slowly down the road. Lancelot was driving. Granny was standing on the back seat behind him, searching for me with a telescope. She looked like a granny version of Lord Nelson.

I waved my arms and shouted. 'Over here, over here!' She waved back and almost tumbled off the bike. She grabbed wildly at Lancelot, first of all clonking him on the helmet with the telescope and then almost pulling his head off in her struggle to keep her balance. He just managed to avoid driving straight into Woolworths.

It was only when they had almost reached me
that I realized they had a passenger in the sidecar.
It was Rubbish, my goat.

'Couldn't leave her behind,' explained Lancelot
as he hugged me. 'Nobody there to milk her so I

thought I might as well bring her along. She could be useful.'

'Really?'

'She can help us track them down,' he explained.

'Really?' I repeated.

'Goats have an excellent sense of smell. I brought some of the babies' clothes with me. She sniffs them and then we set her off on the scent trail, like a bloodhound.'

I opened my mouth to speak. 'And don't say "Really?" again, as if you don't believe it. You've got to believe it, Nick. It's our best chance of finding them. Just let her stretch her legs for a bit.'

I nodded. If Lancelot said it was a good thing to do then it was. It was just that it sounded more like one of my dad's crazy ideas.

Granny pressed a paper bag into my hand. 'These are for you,' she beamed. I looked inside and smiled back at her.

'Thanks, Gran.' She'd brought me two buns.

8 All the Thrill of the Chase

Rubbish was so pleased to see me. I was quite pleased to see her too, but she was drawing a lot of attention to us. It wasn't just Rubbish who was getting odd looks, either. People were staring suspiciously at Granny and Lancelot. I wasn't

surprised because they were in their full bike gear – leather trousers and leather jackets with fringes on the sleeves. Lancelot used to be in the Hell's Angels when he was young and now he had studs all over the back of his jacket that spelled out the words:

MAD, BAD AND ARTHRITIC

Granny's only said: FOSSIL. But I think that might have been the make of the jacket.

A mother brought her little boy over to have a look at Rubbish.

'Wabbit,' he said, and his mother laughed.

'Don't be silly, darling. It's a sheep.'

Lancelot looked at me, winked and put a finger to his lips. 'I think we'd better get going,' he said. 'Hop in with the sheep, Nick. Your crash hat's in there somewhere. Which way did the tour bus take off?'

I pointed in the right direction and off we went. Granny was at the controls this time so that Lancelot could use his mobile. Granny had won motorbike races when she was young. It's true! My granny – a motorbike champion!

Lancelot shouted at me as we headed out of town. 'I'm not just counting on Rubbish. I've got a few motorcycling mates from the old days. I've put out a call. They're looking for the tour bus. Somebody's bound to spot a big thing like that.'

He was right. His phone began to ring and soon we were on the trail. My heart was lifting. It felt as if things had started to go our way and we were closing in. Mind you, I had no idea what we'd do once we'd tracked the giant babies down. Supposing they'd laid a trap? Supposing they were armed? Memories of my dream came flooding back – nappy-bombs and dummies whizzing past my head like bullets. Maybe the traps would turn out to be pits filled with stewed apples.

Lancelot seemed to be on the mobile all the time now. Every so often he would lean forward and shout something to Granny. It was astonishing how she seemed able to hear what he said perfectly well even with a constant gale rushing past her ears as she flew down the road.

At last we stopped. We pulled off our helmets. I looked around but I couldn't see any sign of the tour bus or people. We seemed to be in the middle of nowhere.

'This is where the last sighting was,' Lancelot murmured. 'A mate said he passed it here only half an hour ago. It's time for Rubbish to do her stuff.'

We got the goat out of the sidecar and held some of the twins' clothes up to her nose. 'How will she know what to do?' I asked.

'You're going to tell her. She's your goat, Nick. She knows your voice best. When you're milking her you talk to her all the time, I know. Just tell her what you want her to do – and keep your fingers crossed.'

I bent down and spoke quietly into one of Rubbish's big, hairy ears. 'Find Cheese and Tomato. This is what they smell like. We must find them, Rubbish. Go and find them – now.'

I stood back. Rubbish looked at me, turned round and took two steps backwards so she was standing on my feet and pushed her rear at me, slapping me with her tail. I looked glumly across at Lancelot and Granny.

'What's the matter?' asked Granny.

'She wants to be milked,' I said hopelessly. 'She always does that backing movement and whisking her tail when she needs milking.'

'Best milk her then,' said Lancelot.

'Did you bring a bucket?'

Lancelot slapped his forehead crossly. 'I thought I was being pretty clever bringing the goat. I never thought I'd need a milking bucket as well.'

'She has to be milked into something. She'll have a fit if she sees me squirting it all over the ground.'

Granny silently handed me
her crash hat.

Fifteen minutes later we
set off, with Granny gingerly
carrying a helmet full of
goat's milk. She couldn't bear

to throw it away. 'The crash hat will be all right
after a good wash,' she said hopefully.

'You deserve a medal, babe,' grinned Lancelot.
'A medal for services to goats.'

'Hurry up, you two,' I called to them. 'Rubbish
is on to something.'

Rubbish had picked up speed and was almost
galloping across a field, straight towards a group
of old farm buildings. Sure enough, we shortly

spotted the tour bus,
carefully parked
between the buildings
so that it was almost
completely hidden

away. I grabbed Rubbish and told her to keep still. Lancelot was right beside me. We had to wait while Granny caught up. She couldn't run fast because she was busy trying not to let the goat's milk spill out of her helmet.

'Get rid of it, before it turns to yoghurt,' hissed Lancelot, but she shook her head defiantly and clutched the crash hat closer to her chest.

'I can't bear to. It's such a waste.'

We peered round the corner of a building at the bus. There was no sign of anyone on board. The giant babies had probably taken their prisoners off to one of the other buildings.

'Everything's falling to pieces,' I whispered to Lancelot.

'Must be an abandoned farm,' he muttered back.

'What are we going to do?'

'We need to work out which one of these buildings they're in.'

'It's that one,' Granny interrupted. She pointed across the mucky yard to what looked like a large garage, but could have been almost anything.

'How do you know?' I asked.

'Because there are voices coming from it. Listen.'

Lancelot and I strained our ears. Every so often, if the wind was in the right direction and we stretched out our ears by pulling them with our fingers, a faint sound reached us that could have been someone talking. Granny was right!

'How can you possibly hear that?' I asked.

'You're supposed to be half deaf!'

'I know, dear, and I am, but as you get older your ears play funny tricks on you, and sometimes you become very sensitive to sound in a way that ordinary people aren't.'

Lancelot shook his head in admiration. 'That's my babe! You just got yourself another medal! Come on, keep low and don't make a sound. Nick, you're in charge of the goat. She's our secret weapon – if we need one.'

'She won't get hurt, will she?'

'No, but she might well hurt one of those giant babies.' He stopped for a second and frowned.

'Are you sure they're giant babies? I know you keep calling them that but it does seem odd, Nick.'

I nodded grimly. 'Giant babies, you'll see.'

And he did, because when we reached the shed and peered in through a dirty window, we were met with an unexpected and astonishing sight.

9 Chaaaarge!

It was a classroom. At least that's what it looked like. A few tables had been placed in a row, like desks. Hanging on the wall in front of the desks was a white screen. A PowerPoint display was on show. Obviously there was some kind of lesson going on. Who were the pupils? Guess!

Mum, Dad, Cheese and Tomato, and David

Dumper. Who was the teacher? Guess again!

It's a bit of a trick question because there were three teachers. Exactly. You've got it. The giant babies, still in their nappies and T-shirts.

Outside the window Granny's eyes boggled. 'What *is* going on?'

'I don't know and I don't care,' Lancelot answered. 'It's time to rescue everyone.'

'What's the plan, dear?' asked Granny.

'It's quite simple. We burst in, surprise them and take over. I'll nobble the biggest baby and Nicholas can set Rubbish on the middle one and you go for the woman. We have the element of surprise on our side. My guess is they'll give up without much of a struggle.'

'Suppose they don't?' Granny asked and Lancelot frowned back at her.

'They will,' he insisted. 'Now, on the count of three. One, two, three – CHAAAARGE!'

We burst through the door. Instant chaos! Lancelot hurled himself at the biggest baby and floored him with a rugby tackle. Rubbish and I cornered the other man, with Rubbish doing her best ever impression of a snarling guard dog. It might even have been a bloodhound. As for Granny, she hurried up to the lady baby as fast as she could. For a brief moment they eyeballed each other, then Granny lifted her crash hat and tipped the contents all over her. The lady baby collapsed in a puddle of goat's milk and burst into tears.

'Poo pants!' laughed Tomato, pointing at the baby on the floor.

I turned and grinned triumphantly at Mum, Dad and the others. They didn't look the least bit impressed. In fact they looked almost angry. No, not *almost* angry. They *were* angry! Mr Dumper rose from behind his desk, red-faced and wagging a finger at us.

'Do you mind not interrupting? We'd just got to an interesting bit.' He glanced at the screen. I could see a picture of a grubby white mountain. I could see it wasn't a proper mountain, not a rocky one. It was a mountain of . . . nappies!

Now it was Mum who was eyeing us sternly. 'Did you know this country throws away more than eight million nappies *every day*?'

Well actually, yes, I did.

'Did you know it takes five hundred years for each of those nappies to decompose?' demanded Dad. Well actually, yes, I did. In fact I'd only spoken to him about it the day before. Sometimes parents can be very forgetful. Mr Dumper had more to say.

'Did you know that every disposable nappy is made from one cup of oil? So that makes eight million cups of oil every day, just for this country, let alone the rest of the world. I have never heard of such waste!'

What? Mr Dumper, the disposable-nappy maker, was lecturing me! I wasn't having that. It wasn't fair. I cleared my throat.

'But, Mr Dumper, you're the one who makes disposable pants.'

He shook his head violently. 'Not any more, I don't. Thanks to Biff and Chip here I have discovered things about throwaway nappies that I never knew before. I am going to stop production.'

'Good for you,' said Mum. 'Lancelot, would you take your big biker's boot off Kipper's stomach and help him up? Thank you.'

My head was spinning. What was going on? First of all my family gets kidnapped by giant babies and now they all seem to be best friends. Not only that, but Mr Dumper was going to stop making disposable pants. So he wouldn't be advertising them any more. So there'd be no more shows. So he wouldn't need Cheese any more. Or us.

It felt like a huge hole had opened beneath my feet and I was falling fast.

10 Kristal Brings Good Fortune

We're back at the hotel. We came back on the tour bus, apart from Granny and Lancelot, of course. They were on the bike. Rubbish was with us. She liked the tour bus. I guess it'll be our last night of luxury. Granny and Lancelot are here too, although they almost didn't get in. The hotel were a bit sniffy about allowing what looked like two Hell's Angels to book in, even if they were old-age pensioners.

'I promise we won't trash your hotel,' Lancelot told the receptionist. 'I gave up doing that last year.'

'He's teasing you, dear,' Granny said reassuringly, as a look of panic crossed the poor woman's face. 'Now then, we shall need a bit of straw for the goat.'

The receptionist had a sudden fit of choking. 'Goat?' she eventually managed to splutter.

'Yes, dear. Her name's Rubbish. I'll sign her in if you like. She can't write yet.'

There was no blood left in the receptionist's face. It had all run away in horror. 'I'm very sorry, madam. We don't allow animals in the hotel.'

I know it was a horrible thing for me to do because I already felt very sorry for the poor woman, but I couldn't let this go. 'Excuse me, you've got four dogs staying here. They were barking most of the night. Rubbish doesn't bark. She's a quiet goat, almost silent.'

Rubbish, the almost silent goat, chose that moment to start eating the Visitors' Book lying on top of the reception desk. The receptionist tried

to pull it from her and Rubbish bleated loudly. Everyone in the room stared at her.

'I'm sorry, but we can't take a goat.'

Mr Dumper stepped in. 'We've had a hard day,' he explained to the manager, who had now joined the receptionist at the desk. 'We've been kidnapped by giant babies, been given a long lecture on nappy production and been rescued by these . . .' Mr Dumper broke off, unsure how he should describe Granny and Lancelot. '. . . by these kind people. Would you please give them a room? The goat's part of the team.'

'I'm sorry,' said the manager, who evidently did not believe a word Mr Dumper had said. Kidnapped by giant babies? Don't be ridiculous. I could tell he was thinking exactly that. 'The hotel doesn't have guest rooms for goats.'

'She could stay in our bathroom,' I suggested.

'Good idea, kiddo,' Lancelot grinned.

'Then it won't matter if she does a . . . you

know. Not that she will,' I added hastily. 'She's already been.'

'No goats,' repeated the receptionist.

The entrance doors swung wide and Kristal Gaze came swanning in with her yappy dogs. She started across the hallway, saw Rubbish and stopped dead in her tracks. She lifted her sunglasses to see more clearly. It was as if she couldn't believe her eyes. This was it. Kristal came hurrying across to the desk. She was going to make a fuss, and she did.

'Darlings! My prediction has come true!' She pointed straight at the manager. 'You're the Crab, aren't you?'

'I beg your pardon, madam?'

'You're the Crab, the zodiac sign – Cancer, the Crab?'

'Madam, you are mistaken. I'm Leo – the Lion.'

'I'm Nellie the Elephant,' muttered Dad, but I don't think anyone heard but me.

The receptionist said that she was born under the sign of Cancer. Kristal was delighted. 'I knew it. It was in my prediction for Cancer today. "Something hairy will upset you, but ignore it at your peril. It brings you good fortune." And here you see it,' she went on, pointing at

Rubbish. 'Something hairy. The goat must stay.'

'But, madam –' began the manager. Kristal's eyes turned to hard steel.

'The goat is staying,' she ordered. The manager took a deep, deep breath.

'Very well,' he said and turned to his

receptionist. 'Put the goat in the suite with this charming family.'

'What a lady!' said Mr Dumper admiringly. Kristal Gaze blushed. She did!

'Thank you, kind sir. Are these your babies? They're so gorgeous!'

Now it was Mr Dumper who went red. 'No. No. I'm not married. This is Cheese and here's Tomato.'

Kristal's hand flew to her mouth. 'Cheese! Of course, I should have known. Why, you're famous, young man.' She turned to Tomato. 'And you too, young lady. You're so pretty.'

Kristal tickled Tomato under her little chin while the rest of us held our breath, waiting for Tomato to say what she always said.

'P . . . p . . . ,' she began. Mum gave up and closed her eyes. 'P . . . pretty!' said Tomato.

'Do let me escort you to your room,' suggested Mr Dumper to Kristal, and off they went,

leaving the rest of us almost speechless.

'I think Mr Dumper rather likes Kristal Gaze,'
Mum said quietly.

'And I think Kristal Gaze rather likes Mr
Dumper,' added Dad. They looked at each other
for a second and then chorused: 'Ooooh!'

Rubbish finished making her entry in the
Visitors' Book and spat the remains out on to the
desk.

'We'll pay for a new one,' Mum offered quickly,

before the manager could complain, but he didn't seem to care any longer. I think he felt that so many awful things had already happened it didn't matter if there was one more.

It was good to get to our room. I collapsed into an armchair. I asked Mum and Dad if they were going to report the giant babies to the police. Mum shook her head.

'We've already discussed that with Mr Dumper. They didn't do any harm – just gave us a bit of a shock really. The worst thing they did was leave you behind, and they didn't mean to do that. They thought you were already on the bus, and once they'd grabbed us they could hardly go back and look for you. The really big shock was finding out about disposable nappies.'

'What's going to happen to us?'

'Cheese will get paid for this bit of the roadshow and that'll be it.' Dad sighed. 'It's been good while it lasted, but we always knew it couldn't go on forever. We're just as disposable as the nappies.'

'I wish it could have gone on longer.' It had been such an exciting day and here I was feeling like a wet Monday. I wanted to hide away somewhere dark.

'I'm going to bed,' I announced. And I did. It was only half past six.

11 New Pants!

I slept like a log last night. I was so deeply asleep
I don't think I even dreamed. I only woke up
because something wet and sloppy was being
stuck in my ear – and the something wet and
sloppy had a goat attached to the other end of it.
It was Rubbish's tongue.

'Urrrgh!' I shuddered, leaping out of bed.

'She'd make an excellent alarm clock,' said Mum. 'I wonder if I could get her to do that when you're late for school.'

'Don't even think about it,' I warned. 'She's my goat and she does what I say.'

'And you're my son and you do what I say,' Mum parroted. 'Get dressed double quick and come down for breakfast. Cheese, I can see you in the bathroom. Stop trying to climb inside the toilet. Nick, go and rescue him, will you? Honestly, you need eyes in the back of your head with those two. Where's Tomato got to now?'

We got safely down to breakfast eventually. Gran and Lancelot were already there but there was no sign of Mr Dumper.

'Perhaps he overslept,' said Mum with a smile.

'Maybe he was up late,' nodded Dad, with a big wink. 'Look, here he comes now, and guess who he's with?'

'Kristal Gaze,' I murmured. 'She's weird.'

'Sssh,' said Mum quickly. 'Don't let her hear
you, they're coming over.'

'Good morning all!' cried Mr Dumper
cheerfully. 'What a wonderful morning it is. Do

you know, I am full of beans and bright ideas. In fact I've been up half the night, thinking. Do you know what I'm going to do?'

We shook our heads. I'm not sure why, because we did know what he was going to do. He was going to stop making Dumpers and dump us.

'I am going to stop making disposable pants.' See? I told you.

'Poo pants!' said Tomato, rather predictably, and it was just what I was thinking. I was getting angry. Everything was poo pants as far as I was concerned.

Mr Dumper beamed at Tomato and went on. 'I'm going to stop producing that disposable stuff and I'm going to start making environmentally friendly nappies. I'm going to make real nappies that can be recycled and you know what I'm going to call them? Rainbow Dumpers! Isn't that great? And do you know why I'm naming them after the rainbow? Because they're going to be all the colours of the rainbow. Just imagine – nappies in full colour. Rainbow Dumpers are going to be new pants for a new world!'

'Noo pants!' cried Tomato, clapping both hands above her head.

Mr Dumper was delighted. 'Say it again! Go on! New pants.'

NOO pants!

'Noo pants!' gurgled Tomato.

Mr Dumper turned to Kristal. 'Isn't she adorable? You know what, that's the angle we need for the new advert. We'll get Tomato on film shouting "Noo pants!" She will be the new face of Rainbow Dumpers. After all, her bottom's just as good as her brother's. She has such a cheeky smile!'

'You think her bottom *smiles*?' asked Dad, a bit surprised.

'He doesn't mean her bottom,' snapped Mum. 'Her face!'

'I want that girl in the next advert,' said Mr Dumper. 'I'll get a contract drawn up at once. And there's something else I'm going to do. You'll never guess. I'm going to get married. Kristal Gaze and I are engaged!'

'Congratulations!' cried Mum, trying to cover up the noise of Dad choking on his toast.

'Well done,' echoed Granny. 'You know,

Lancelot and I got married when we were quite old.'

Kristal's smile froze. 'Excuse me? Are you suggesting I'm old?'

Lancelot leaned across to Granny. 'You're wearing the wrong glasses, babe,' he suggested.

'No, I'm not, I checked before I – ow!' Granny yelped. 'Someone kicked me under the table. Well

I never. Do you know, I think I must have the wrong glasses on. Silly me.'

'It's the sort of thing that happens when you're old,' said Kristal coldly.

'Where's Cheese?' Mum asked. 'Don't tell me he's vanished again.'

'He's vanished again,' I said helpfully.

'Cheese? Cheese? Where are you?'

All at once the bottom of Kristal's long dress was lifted up and a smiley face appeared. 'Boo!' he said.

'Oh!' cried Kristal. 'That's no place to go and hide. What are you doing under there, young man?'

'Pretty,' gurgled Cheese. 'Pretty pants!'

Kristal Gaze turned beetroot. Mr Dumper tried not to burst out laughing but couldn't stop himself. Mum gathered up Cheese and muttered an apology. Granny and Lancelot hid their smiles and I tried hard to stare at the ceiling because I

knew if I looked at any of their faces I'd burst into uncontrollable giggles.

It's all worked out quite well really, especially as Mr Dumper doesn't just want Tomato as the new

Cheese – he wants Dad to work for him too. You see, my dad has finally come up with some good ideas.

'The thing is,' he told Mr Dumper, 'you needn't stop at nappies that are different colours. They could have writing on them.'

'How do you mean?' asked Mr Dumper.

'Like you see on T-shirts,' Dad explained. 'One might say BEWARE – TOXIC FUMES.'

'Oh, I like that,' chuckled Mr Dumper.

'Or you could have TODAY WILL BE WET AND WINDY.'

'Hah! Even better!'

'How about a nappy that says No. 1 on the front, and No. 2 on the back?'

Mr Dumper stopped dead, looked at Dad for a second and burst out laughing. 'Priceless!' he cried. 'You've got to come and work for me. With ideas like those we'll have the whole world buying Rainbow Dumpers. I might even make some big enough for those giant babies!'

I suddenly remembered my nightmare. You remember the one where I was being chased by giant babies and dwarf dogs? Listening to Dad's ideas had given me one of my own.

'Someone ought to make nappies for dogs,' I said quietly, because I was afraid everyone would laugh at me. The room went horribly quiet. They all turned their eyes on me.

'What did you say?' croaked Mr Dumper.

'I said someone ought to make nappies for dogs.'

He studied me for several seconds, slowly shaking his head. At last he spoke. 'I don't believe it. The boy's a genius!'

'The boy's a genius,' echoed Dad. 'Nappies for dogs. What a fantastic idea.'

'I'll call them Doggy-dumps,' smiled Mr Dumper. He turned to Cheese and Tomato. 'What do you say, Cheese? What do you say,

Tomato? What do you think of Doggy-dumps?'

I won't tell you what they said. You already know.

Ask Jeremy

Of all the books you have written, which one is your favourite?

I loved writing both **KRAZY KOW SAVES THE WORLD – WELL, ALMOST** and **STUFF**, my first book for teenagers. Both these made me laugh out loud while I was writing and I was pleased with the overall result in each case. I also love writing the stories about Nicholas and his daft family – **MY DAD**, **MY MUM**, **MY BROTHER** and so on.

If you couldn't be a writer what would you be?

Well, I'd be pretty fed up for a start, because writing was the one thing I knew I wanted to do from the age of nine onward. But if I DID have to do something else, I would love to be either an accomplished pianist or an artist of some sort. Music and art have played a big part in my whole life and I would love to be involved in them in some way.

What's the best thing about writing stories?

Oh dear – so many things to say here! Getting paid for making things up is pretty high on the list! It's also something you do on your own, inside your own head – nobody can interfere with that. The only boss you have is yourself. And you are creating something that nobody else has made before you. I also love making my readers laugh and want to read more and more.

Did you ever have a nightmare teacher? (And who was your best ever?)

My nightmare at primary school was Mrs Chappell, long since dead. I knew her secret – she was not actually human. She was a Tyrannosaurus rex in disguise. She taught me for two years when I was in Y5 and Y6, and we didn't like each other at all. My best ever was when I was in Y3 and Y4. Her name was Miss Cox, and she was the one who first encouraged me to write stories. She was brilliant. Sadly, she is long dead too.

When you were a kid you used to play kiss-chase. Did you always do the chasing or did anyone ever chase you?!

I usually did the chasing, but when I got chased, I didn't bother to run very fast! Maybe I shouldn't admit to that! We didn't play kiss-chase at school – it was usually played during holidays. If we had tried playing it at school we would have been in serious trouble. Mind you, I seemed to spend most of my time in trouble of one sort or another, so maybe it wouldn't have mattered that much.

Woofy hi! I'm Streaker, the fastest dog in the world. My owner, Trevor, thinks he can train me to obey him. The trouble is even I don't know what I'm going to do next! I don't know what **SIT** or **STOP** mean, and I do get into some big scrapes. We almost got arrested once! This is the first book about me and it's almost as funny and fast as I am!

LAUGH YOUR SOCKS OFF with

THE HUNDRED-MILE-AN-HOUR DOG

Available Now!

★ ★ ★ ★ ★ ★ ★ ★ ★ ★ ★ ★ ★ ★ ★ ★ ★ ★

I'm Jamie. I am going to be the world's greatest film director when I grow up. I'm trying to make a film about a cartoon cow I've invented called **KRAZY KOW**. However, making a film isn't as easy as you might think. How was I to know everyone would see the bit where I caught my big sister snogging Justin? How was I to know the exploding strawberries would make quite so much mess? How was I to know my big bro's football kit would turn pink? And why did everyone have to blame ME?

LAUGH YOUR SOCKS OFF with

KRAZY KOW SAVES THE WORLD – WELL, ALMOST

Available Now!